# The Pit

by Linda Hoy

Illustrated by Ann Baum

# Contents

# The Story Begins . . .

Ben ran inside the gift shop as it began
to rain. There were lots of good things
for sale, but Ben only had enough
money for some chocolate.

Everyone was waiting for the next tour round the cave.

"This way, please!" They all walked towards the entrance.

"My name's Emma and I'm your tour guide for this afternoon."

Ben had no ticket and no money but everyone else had already paid.

Emma hadn't noticed. "Follow me," she said.

Ben thought he would be warm and dry inside the cave. He thought he could have a free tour. He thought he would not be noticed among the big crowd of people. But Ben didn't know that – in front of him – was the most terrifying journey of his life …

# CHAPTER 1

# Into the Pit

Ben held his breath. The ghostly shape crept closer and closer towards him. The cave was dark, pitch black, so how could he see this figure looming out of the darkness? Ben tried to speak but no words came. He stood open-mouthed and trembling as the ghostly glow edged nearer and nearer.

"Well, that's what it's like if we turn off the lights," said Emma. "Put your hand in front of your face. Move your fingers. I bet you can't see them."

Ben raised his shaking fingers. He held them in front of his face. Emma was right. He could see nothing. Nothing but black. When he wiggled his fingers, he saw nothing at all.

But he could still see the glow of light edging towards him like something out of a nightmare. Real and not real. Visible but . . . An icy tremor made Ben's flesh crawl.

Ghostly fingers were reaching towards him. He saw them – pale as moonlight – as they touched his hand. He felt them, clammy and cold, as they crawled across his skin.

"W. . .w. . .w. . .w. . ." Ben's mouth opened and closed. His jaw shook. He could not speak. His fingers trembled. He reached his hand into the dark but the space in front of him was empty. There was no one there at all.

"There!" Emma switched the light back on.

Now Ben could see. He was standing by a deep black hole. He peered inside but there was nothing there. Just a deep, deep, empty drop. He looked around. No one else was near. So who had touched him in the darkness? Whose were the icy fingers pressing on his hand?

"A long time ago," said Emma, "children worked here in the mine. They were lowered down this long drop here . . ." – she pointed – ". . . into the mine where they worked all day. They crawled along the narrow tunnels in the dark, dragging heavy buckets."

"Didn't they have any light?" someone asked.

"Only candles," said Emma. "One boy had the job of holding the candle to light the way for everyone."

At the back of the cave was a giant rock.

"Can you see up there?" asked Emma.

"There's a platform. The miners carved that
platform and these steps." She pointed to the
steps carved into the stone. "The miners
carved the steps so that they could escape if

the river ever flooded. Listen . . ."

They all stood still and listened.

"Can you hear the river?"

A long way in the distance, Ben could hear
rushing water.

"That's the underground river. When the miners heard the water, they knew they were safe. When the river began to flood, the sound of the water stopped. The water would rise silently higher and higher until it reached the tunnel.

"You see," Emma explained, "the hill above us has lots of caves and potholes and, when it rains, the water runs inside. It fills up even the biggest caves."

"Did any of the miners ever drown?" asked someone.

"Yes," said Emma. "There was a boy called Dan who was only ten years old. His job was to hold the candle to light the way for the miners.

"One day, the underground river fell silent. The miners called the alarm. Dan was supposed to wait for them, holding the candle to show the way out. But he was scared. When the alarm was raised, he ran and ran and got lost inside the tunnels. The miners got out just as the cave began to flood. Then they realized that Dan was left behind. No one dared go back because the water was too high.

"The next day, the miners returned to the cave but the water was even higher. It was six days before the water went down. When the miners searched the cave, they didn't think Dan would still be alive but they shouted his name: 'Dan! Dan!'

"No one answered.

"Later, the miners found a pile of rocks and rubble. The force of the water had moved the stones and there had been an avalanche. Peeping from under the rocks they saw the small stick of a candle. They scraped away at the rubble. Then they found Dan's body. His leg had been trapped by the avalanche. When the flood water came, he couldn't run away. He had drowned.

"Now," called Emma. "Follow me. We're going back up through the tunnel." Everyone set off.

Ben was still shaking. He was scared. He still wondered what had touched him in the darkness. He could not forget the icy fingers creeping across his skin.

"Mind your heads!" called Emma. "The roof gets very low just here."

Ben ran to catch up. He saw everyone bending low as they crept along the narrow tunnel.

"Not far now."

But Ben ran much too fast. He ran straight into the low arch of the tunnel and ...
BANG! He hit his head against the rock.

He saw red stars and yellow lights. He saw white circles, swirling. He tried to shout but his mouth just opened and closed. He fell backwards over a pile of rocks. Then the rocks began to slide under his feet.

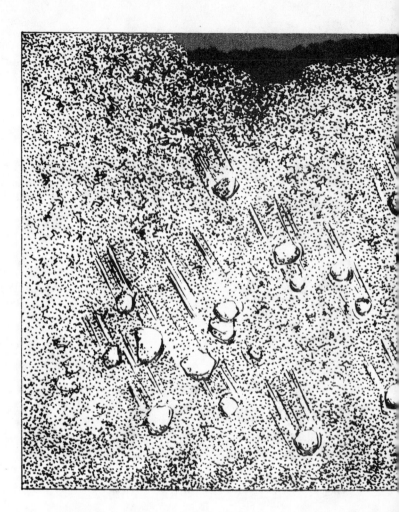

Ben stumbled off the path. He fell down,
down, down. Down into the empty darkness.
He grabbed a big stone but it came away in
his hand. He grazed his fingers as he struggled

to claw his way back up. He scratched his
arms as he slid further and further down. His
stomach lurched.

A wave of terror flooded over him as he fell into the empty blackness. Down into the empty pit.

There was a rushing sound, then a heavy thud. Ben landed on a pile of stones.

From a long way off, he could hear Emma's voice, but it was very, very faint. Ben tried again to shout but his strength was gone. He closed his eyes.

The circles of white light were still there, swirling round and round . . . and that was the last thing he remembered.

It was a long time later when Ben woke up. Where was he?

He blinked. Everything was black. He could see nothing at all. What had happened?

The blackness pressed against him, suffocating him. Where was he? His head hurt. He felt sick and dizzy. He was shivering with cold. *What had happened?*

Plop! A drop of icy water landed on his head. Ben tried to move but his arms and legs were stuck.

Plop! Another drop of water landed on Ben's neck. It trickled down his back. He tried again to move but his hands and arms were too sore.

Ben listened. From a long, long way away, he heard a clanking sound like a heavy gate being closed. There was another sound as well, like a river rushing in the distance.

Then Ben remembered Emma's words: *When the miners heard the water, they knew they were safe . . .*

Of course, he was still inside the cave. He remembered running towards the tunnel and bumping his head.

Plop! Another drop of water landed on Ben's nose. He tried again to lever himself on to his elbows, but he didn't have the strength.

Perhaps if he just sat there and waited,

Emma would come back. She would notice that he was missing before she left the cave. Surely she would count everyone? They wouldn't lock up the cave with someone left inside.

# CHAPTER 2

# Echoes of Fear

Upstairs, Emma was ready to go home. The entrance to the cave was locked with a heavy iron gate. Bill, who looked after the shop, was locking up and taking the money to the bank.

"Busy day?" he asked Emma.

Emma looked at the numbers on her tickets. "Not bad."

"Has everyone gone home?"

27

Emma looked at her tickets again. She had sold two hundred and ten. She looked at the numbers on the gate. Two hundred and ten people had left the cave. "That's right," said Emma. "Everyone's gone."

Bill put his cap on. "It's still raining," he said. "If it carries on like this, the cave might flood. We might not be able to open it tomorrow."

Emma grinned. "Never mind," she told him. "I'll be glad to have a lie-in for a change."

Plop! Another drop of water fell on Ben's head. It trickled down his neck. He tried again to move. His arms hurt and his hands were sore, but it was his leg that hurt him most. He had fallen with his left leg twisted beneath him. When Ben moved his leg, the pain was like a knife twisting in his flesh. He kept still instead. Perhaps he would be rescued soon.

Ben listened but heard nothing. Where was the next group of visitors? They would come past soon with Emma, he thought. He would shout for help when he heard voices. They would hear him and lift him out.

Then, Ben remembered his chocolate. He was glad he hadn't eaten it already. He pulled the bar out of his pocket, tore off the wrapper and ate the chocolate very, very slowly. He wanted to make it last. It was the best chocolate he had ever tasted.

After the chocolate, there was nothing else to do. Ben couldn't move his arms or his legs. He just waited and waited. Where was Emma? Why hadn't she come back?

Ben listened. He strained his ears but heard nothing. Nothing at all. Sometimes there was a plop of water but no footsteps. No voices. He took a deep breath.

"Help!" he shouted. "Is anybody there?"

"Anybody there?" called a voice.

Ben felt better already. "Yes," he shouted back. "I'm here."

"Here!" said the distant voice.

"I've fallen down the pit!" shouted Ben.

But the voice answered, "The pit, the pit . . ." Ben realized that it was only an echo.

"Help!"

"Help . . . help . . ."

"Is anybody there?"

"Anybody there . . . there . . . there . . ."

Ben took a long deep breath. There didn't seem any point in shouting. But what else could he do?

# CHAPTER 3

# A Watery Grave?

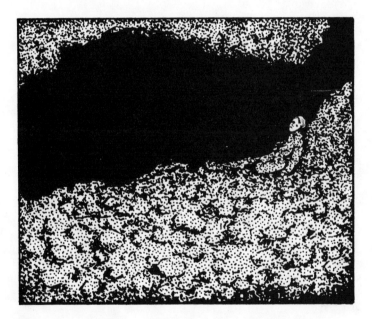

A long time passed. Ben knew something was wrong. He had a watch but he couldn't see it in the dark. He knew it was getting late, though. Might the cave be closed?

Ben knew his mum would be getting worried. He ought to be home by now.

But Ben's mum didn't know where he was. She didn't know he had gone inside the cave. She wouldn't know where to start looking for him.

Ben listened again. He strained his ears for the sound of footsteps, voices, or . . .

Suddenly, he began to feel scared. Cold sweat trickled from his forehead. He realized that the sound of the river had stopped. Not just now, but a long time ago.

The rush of water had been there in the background before. And now it had stopped.

But when? And why hadn't he noticed it before?

What was it Emma had said?

*The hill above us has lots of caves and potholes and, when it rains, the water runs inside. It fills up even the biggest caves.*

Of course, it had started raining many hours ago. That was why Ben had sheltered in the shop. Why hadn't he realized the danger? And what if it was still raining? That could be why there were no more groups of people. The cave would close early because the rain would make it dangerous.

What else had Emma said?

*When the river began to flood, the sound of the water stopped. The water would rise*

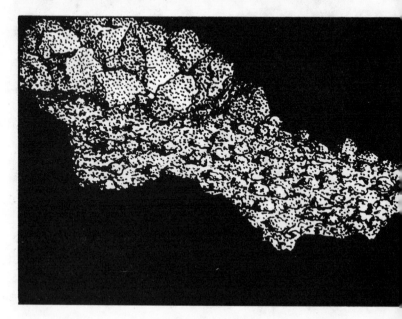

*silently higher and higher until it reached the tunnel.*

Ben reached his right foot as far down as he could. It still seemed dry. But the drips of water from the roof were faster now. Ben's head was soaking wet.

He knew that he would have to move. He couldn't just stay there and drown. No matter how much pain he was in, Ben would have to find a way to crawl out of the pit.

# CHAPTER 4

# A Light in the Darkness

Ben knew his left leg must be broken. It had twisted underneath him when he fell. If he put any weight on it, the pain made him scream.

Ben's hands and arms were sore, but they could take his weight. So, he began to crawl along the stony ground, slowly and painfully, using his hands and his right knee.

The skin was torn from his fingers; his knee was grazed and sore. Ben carried on, hoping to find a way out. Hoping to see some light. But all he could see was darkness.

Suddenly, Ben found his hands squelching in icy water. Instead of crawling up towards the entrance, he'd been going downhill, down towards the river.

"Help!" Ben shouted. "Is anybody there?"

"Anybody there?" came the echo.

"Anybody there . . .?"

"I'm here. At the bottom of the pit!"

"Bottom of the pit," the echo answered.

"Pit . . . pit . . . pit . . ."

Ben knew he would have to turn round and crawl back. He must get back to the entrance before the river filled the cave.

Ben turned around and began his painful journey. Every movement jarred his broken leg. Sharp stones cut his hands. They tore the skin off his fingers. And now, the river was rising.

Whenever Ben stopped to rest, he felt the water lapping at his feet. He had to get away; if he rested too long he would drown.

Slowly and painfully, Ben dragged himself along the tunnel, back to the place where he had fallen. He stopped for a few seconds to get his breath. He remembered Emma's story about Dan, the boy who had drowned in the cave. He had drowned when his leg was trapped by a rock. Ben was determined that wouldn't happen to him.

He would keep going, no matter how bad the pain. Sooner or later, he would find a light showing the way to the entrance. Sooner or later, he would get home alive.

It took Ben a long, long time to climb out of the pit. The rocks and stones he used to pull himself up kept coming away in his hands. The water was rising fast. Every time he fell back, he got wetter and wetter. Now his feet were squelching. His jeans were soaked. Even his shirt was soaked with the water trickling from the roof straight down his neck.

Ben lay on the path and had a rest. He felt exhausted. All he wanted was to go to sleep. But he knew he mustn't stay there. He had to carry on.

The problem was – which way?

Ben tried hard to remember where he was when he fell. Which way did the others go? Which way was the entrance? He wasn't sure. He set off crawling forwards, hoping to see a light.

Ten minutes later, Ben found himself back at the river again. He had crawled along the narrow tunnel, hoping to find a light. But all he found was the river rising silently in the darkness. Now, he felt like crying. He just wanted to lie down and go to sleep, to let the water seep over him. But he mustn't drown. He turned around, dragging his broken leg behind him again, seeking out flat, dry earth with his torn fingers.

Instead of crying, he talked to himself, "I must get out," he said. "I must get out . . ."

And all around him the cavern answered back, "Must get out . . . must get out . . ."

As he dragged himself forward, Ben spoke again, but louder: "I must get out!" he insisted. "I must get out!"

And this time the answer came loud and strong, "Must get out! Must get out . . ."

Ben arrived back at the tunnel, the place where he had bumped his head. But by now, his mind was in turmoil. He couldn't remember the way back. He crawled about on his hands and knees. There was one passage here, another tunnel here, another path here . . . which one should he take? Ben sat down on a rock. The water was now flowing into the cave.

He wouldn't be able to crawl any further. The water would reach his chin.

"Which way shall I go now?" he shouted. "Which way?"

"Which way . . .? Which way . . .? Which way . . .?" came the echo.

And then there was something else. A pinprick of light in the distance.

CHAPTER 5

# A Ghostly Helper

At first, Ben's heart leapt. Perhaps he was much closer to the entrance than he thought.

But the spot of light was moving. It came nearer and nearer. A rescuer perhaps? "Hello!" shouted Ben. "Hello."

"Hello," the cave echoed. "Hello . . ."

It might be a potholer or Emma or the man who took the money in the shop. But why didn't the person holding the light say anything?

"Hello there," said Ben. He tried to make his voice sound friendly but it came out like a squeak. "Hello . . ."

"Hello . . ." Even the cave sounded terrified of the approaching glimmer of light.

Then Ben realized. He had seen the light before. His heart stopped beating for a moment. He held his breath. This was exactly the same shape he had seen when Emma turned off the light.

This was the frightening phantom that had touched him in the dark and now it was here. But this time he was alone.

There was no one else to turn to. Emma wasn't here to switch the light back on and, of course, he couldn't run away. The tunnel was filled with water.

"W. . .w. . .who are you?" asked Ben as the strange shape got nearer. His voice was no more than a whisper.

This time, there was no echo but Ben could see clearly. Emerging from the strange light was a figure. The outline of a boy. The boy looked younger than Ben, with a pale face and old-fashioned ragged clothes. He was holding a small hollow stone in his hand.

Inside the stone was a candle. It was the candle that gave the light.

The strange boy came nearer. Ben could smell his dirty, unwashed clothes. He could smell the candle wax. The boy's hair was long and greasy, tied back with string. Ben stood rooted to the spot. The two boys stared at each other. Ben wondered if he ought to say something, but he was much too scared to speak.

Then the boy raised his candle, lighting the cave above their heads. Ben looked around: there was the tunnel where he had bumped his head; there was the path and there was the river, creeping now around their knees.

The strange boy set off along the path, holding the candle up high. The last thing Ben wanted was to follow him. But what else could he do? He couldn't stay in the cave and drown.

The water was now too deep for him to crawl. Ben leant his arms against the wall, hopped a step and rested, hopped a step and rested, hopped and . . .

He couldn't go much further. But the boy was waiting for him and, as he watched, Ben noticed something. The strange boy also had something wrong with his leg. He couldn't walk properly either. Then Ben remembered Emma's story again. Could this be the ghost of Dan, the boy who had drowned when his leg was trapped in the cave?

Had he come back from the dead to help Ben find the way to safety?

Or had this ghost appeared just because Ben was nearly dead himself. Perhaps that was why Ben could see him – perhaps he would die as well. Perhaps both of them would be ghosts, haunting the cave together . . .

After a while, the boy held the candle higher. He seemed to be floating upwards.

Ben could hardly move another step. The water had now reached his waist and every step took a massive effort. Ben was terrified of falling into the water. He knew that if he fell now, he wouldn't have the strength to get back up.

Then Ben saw the steps. The boy was shining his candle on the steps carved in the rock. Ben remembered the steps that the miners dug – their route to safety when the river flooded.

Ben staggered forward. His clothes were heavy with water. He was shivering with cold. He knew that, if only he could climb the steps, he would be safe.

But now his strength had gone. He tried to lift his leg on to the first step but the effort was too much.

He fell.

Ben felt the water lapping over him, cool and welcoming. He just wanted to lie there – lie there and go to sleep. Lie there and give up.

But then he felt a tug on his sleeve. Ben looked up. The boy was shining the candle in his face. "Come on," he seemed to be saying. "Come on. You can do it. You can do it if you try."

Ben lifted his head. Then he lifted his arm. Then, slowly and painfully, he lifted his leg. Inch by inch, Ben began to climb. He crawled on his hands and knees, one step at a time. When he thought he could go no further, he reached the very last step. He collapsed at the top with exhaustion.

The ghostly figure had led him all the way.

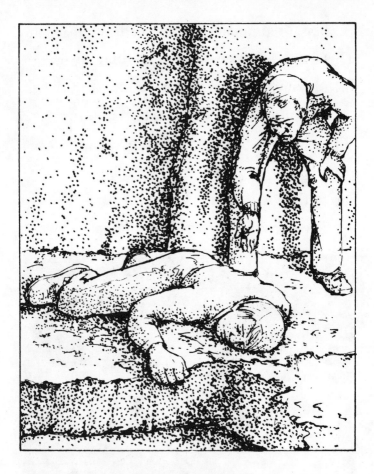

"Ben! Hello! Are you there?"

It was the man from the shop who remembered Ben. He remembered selling him the chocolate.

"Ben! Hello! Are you in there?"

When the police began searching for Ben, the shopkeeper told them he had seen him go inside the cave.

"Can you hear us, Ben?"

"Here. Here I am!"

When the search party found him, he was exhausted, cold and hungry. But he was still alive.

Of course, no one believed Ben's story about the strange boy who had led him to the steps. But no one could explain the hollow stone left at Ben's side.

The stone still had a stub of candle burning inside it, lighting up the cave.